Walter de la Mare

the Turnip

ILLUSTRATED BY
KEVIN HAWKES

DAVID R. GODINE · PUBLISHER · BOSTON

First published in 1992 by
David R. Godine, Publisher, Inc.
Horticultural Hall
300 Massachusetts Avenue
Boston, Massachusetts 02115

Library of Congress Cataloguing-in-Publication Data
De la Mare, Walter, 1873-1956
The turnip / Walter de la Mare ; illustrated by Kevin Hawkes.
p.   cm.
Summary: A kind but poor farmer gains a fortune and his rich
brother's envy when he grows an enormous turnip.
ISBN: 0-87923-934-4
[1. Fairy tales. 2. Folklore—Germany.] I. Hawkes, Kevin, ill. II. Title
PZ8.D37TU 1992
398-21—dc20   92-6191   CIP   AC

THE TURNIP
was set in Monotype Bembo on the Macintosh.
Bembo is based on the types used by the Venetian scholar-publisher
Aldus Manutius in the printing of *De Aetna,* written by Pietro Bembo and
published in 1495. The original characters were cut in 1490 by Francesco Griffo
who, at Aldus's request, later cut the first italic types. Originally adapted by
the English Monotype Company, Bembo is now widely available and
highly regarded. It remains one of the most elegant, readable and
widely used of all book faces. Typesetting and design
by Lucinda Hitchcock.

FIRST EDITION
Printed in Hong Kong by South China Printing Company

the Turnip

ONCE UPON A TIME there were two brothers, or rather half-brothers, for they had had the same father, but different mothers; and no two human beings could be more unlike one another. The elder brother was as sly as a fox, and had no more pity or compassion than a weasel. As he grew up he had always bought cheap and sold dear. He would rub his hands together with joy to lend a poor neighbour money, for he knew he was sure of getting ten times as much paid back. Oh, he was a villain, and no mistake!

Yet he lived in a fine big house full of fine furniture, with stone gate-posts and a high wall all round his garden. He dressed in a gown of velvet, and when he sat down to supper, there were never less than seven different dishes on his table. Up in a high gallery, all set about with wax candles, stood fiddlers playing as fast as they could, until he had finished picking his bones and sopping up his gravy down below.

Yet though this brother was so rich he had very few real friends, and most of such people as might have been his friends hated him, chiefly because he was a mean and merciless greedyguts. The one thing he wanted was to rise in the world and have everybody else bow and scrape before him; and his one inmost hope was that some day the King would hear of him and of all his money, and invite him to come and dine with him at his Palace, and perhaps make him a nobleman. After that, he thought, he could die happy!

THE OTHER BROTHER was as different from this as chalk from cheese. He had nothing more in the world than a meagre little farm, three cows, a sow, a horse in stable too old to work, an ass a few years older, and his chickens, ducks and geese. He worked hard from early morning to night to keep even these. Yet he always seemed to be cheerful and never sick or sorry.

The only time he had ever asked his rich brother for help he got nothing but sneers and insults; and after that the servants set the dogs on to him. Yet he himself would never have turned even a hungry cur from his door — not, at least, if he had a bone in his cupboard. And rather than kill a mouse in a trap he'd carry it off half a mile from the farm to set it free, and then give his old brown house-cat an extra saucer of milk to make up for it.

NOW ONE APRIL EVENING, as this brother was feeding his poultry in the stackyard, suddenly, and as if out of nowhere, an old cross-eyed man popped up his head over the rough wall and asked him for a drink of water.

"Water!" said the farmer. "As much as you like, my friend — to drink, wash, or swim in! But if you'll step inside, I can give you a taste of something with a little more flavour to it."

He led the old man kindly into the kitchen, and having cut him off a plate of good fat bacon and a slice or two of bread, he drew him a jug of cider. It was the best he could give, and the cross-eyed old man, though he ate little, thanked him heartily. And as he was about to go on his way he gave a squint at the sun now low in the west, then another very quick and sharp at the farmer, and asked him if he grew turnips.

The farmer laughed, and said, Ay, he did grow turnips.

"There be some that grow turnips," mumbled the old man, "that wouldn't spare even a blind man a cheese-rind; and there be some — " but here he stopped, and flinging up his hand into the air, he went on in a lingo which the farmer not only could not catch, but the like of which he had never heard before. Then the old man went away, and the farmer thought no more of him.

ONE MORNING A MONTH or two afterwards, the farmer went out to pull a turnip or two for his hot-pot, and noticed up in the northwest corner of his field what looked to be a green tufty bush growing where no sort of bush ought to be. He shaded his eyes with his hand and looked again — and was astonished. But as he drew nearer he saw his mistake, for what he had taken to be a bush was nothing else than what you would most expect in a turnip field — that is to say, a Turnip; but of a size and magnitude the like of which had never been seen in the world before, not even in the island where the people are all giants.

The farmer stood and marvelled. He couldn't take his eyes off this Turnip. It was some little time before he realized that what he was looking at was not only *a* Turnip, but was *his* Turnip. After that, he went off at once and called his neighbours to come. It took them all that day until evening to dig the Turnip out. Early next morning they brought a farm-wagon, and, after scraping off the earth on the root, and washing it down with buckets of water, they managed at last to heave and hoist it into the wagon. Then they rested a bit, to recover their breath.

THE NEXT THING was to decide what to do with the Turnip. There was flesh enough in it to feed an army, and as for "tops," there were enough of them, as one of the farmer's old friends said, to keep a widow and nine children in green-meat for a hundred years on end.

"Oy," said another, "given they didn't rot!"

"Oy," said a third, "biled free!"

"Oy," said a fourth, "and a pinch of salt in the water."

And then they all said, "Oy."

But while his neighbours were talking the farmer was thinking, and while he was thinking he gazed steadily at his Turnip.

"What's in my *mind,* neighbours," he began at last, taking off his hat and scratching his head, "is that turnips is turnips, and of turnips as *such* I've got enough and to spare. But that there monster is, as you might say, not the same thing nohow. That there is a Turnip which for folk like you and me is beyond all boiling, buttering, mashing, ingogitating and consummeration. And what's in my *mind,* friends, is whether you agree with me that maybe His Majesty the King would like to have a look at it?"

The question was not what the farmer's friends had expected. They looked at him, they looked at one another, and last they looked again at the Turnip — the fresh, rain-scented wind now blowing freely in its fronds.

Then altogether, and as if at a signal, they said, "Oy." The next thing was to get the Turnip to the Palace. It took two strapping cart-horses, as well as the farmer's ass harnessed up in front with a length of rope. But even at that, it needed a long pull and a strong pull and a pull altogether, with his neighbours one and all shoving hard on the spokes of the wheels, to get the wagon out of the field.

Once on the high-road, however, it rode easy, and away they went.

Long before the farmer neared the gates of the Palace the streets of the city were buzzing like a beehive. Everyone marvelled. But the people at the windows and on the house-tops saw the Turnip best, for a good deal of the root was hidden by the sides and tailpiece of the wagon, and by the sacks laid over it. When the wagon actually reached the Palace gates, it was surrounded by such a throng and press of people there was scarcely room to sneeze, but there the sentries on guard kept them all back, and the farmer led his ass and two horses into the quiet beyond, alone.

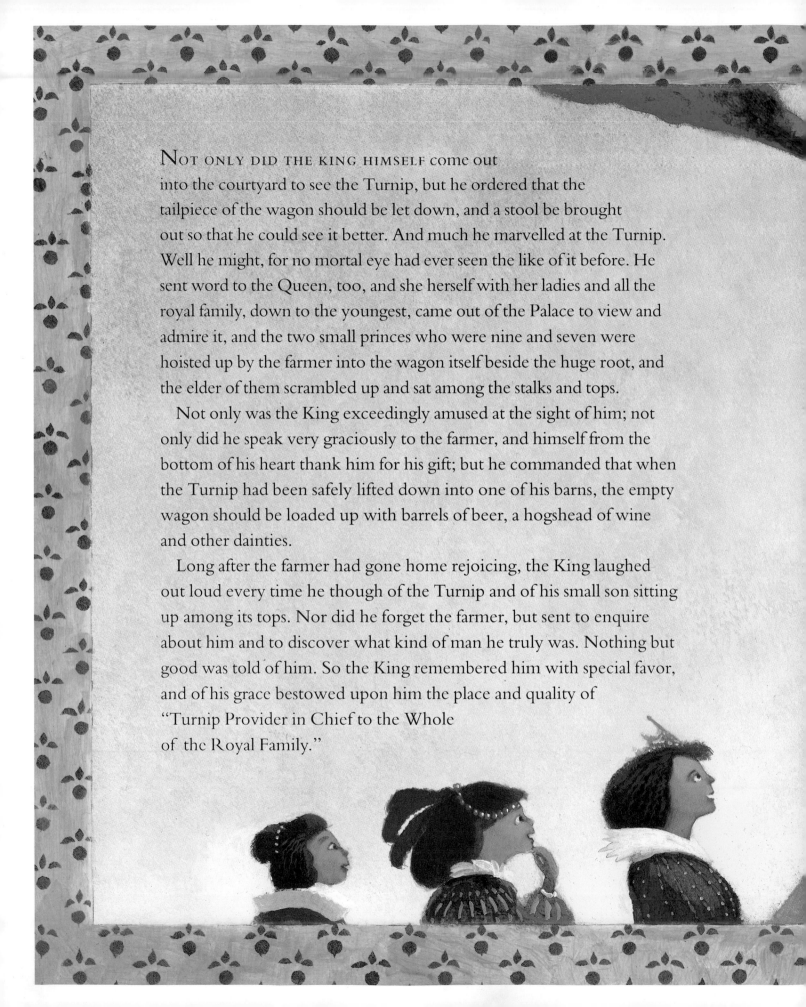

Not only did the king himself come out into the courtyard to see the Turnip, but he ordered that the tailpiece of the wagon should be let down, and a stool be brought out so that he could see it better. And much he marvelled at the Turnip. Well he might, for no mortal eye had ever seen the like of it before. He sent word to the Queen, too, and she herself with her ladies and all the royal family, down to the youngest, came out of the Palace to view and admire it, and the two small princes who were nine and seven were hoisted up by the farmer into the wagon itself beside the huge root, and the elder of them scrambled up and sat among the stalks and tops.

Not only was the King exceedingly amused at the sight of him; not only did he speak very graciously to the farmer, and himself from the bottom of his heart thank him for his gift; but he commanded that when the Turnip had been safely lifted down into one of his barns, the empty wagon should be loaded up with barrels of beer, a hogshead of wine and other dainties.

Long after the farmer had gone home rejoicing, the King laughed out loud every time he though of the Turnip and of his small son sitting up among its tops. Nor did he forget the farmer, but sent to enquire about him and to discover what kind of man he truly was. Nothing but good was told of him. So the King remembered him with special favor, and of his grace bestowed upon him the place and quality of "Turnip Provider in Chief to the Whole of the Royal Family."

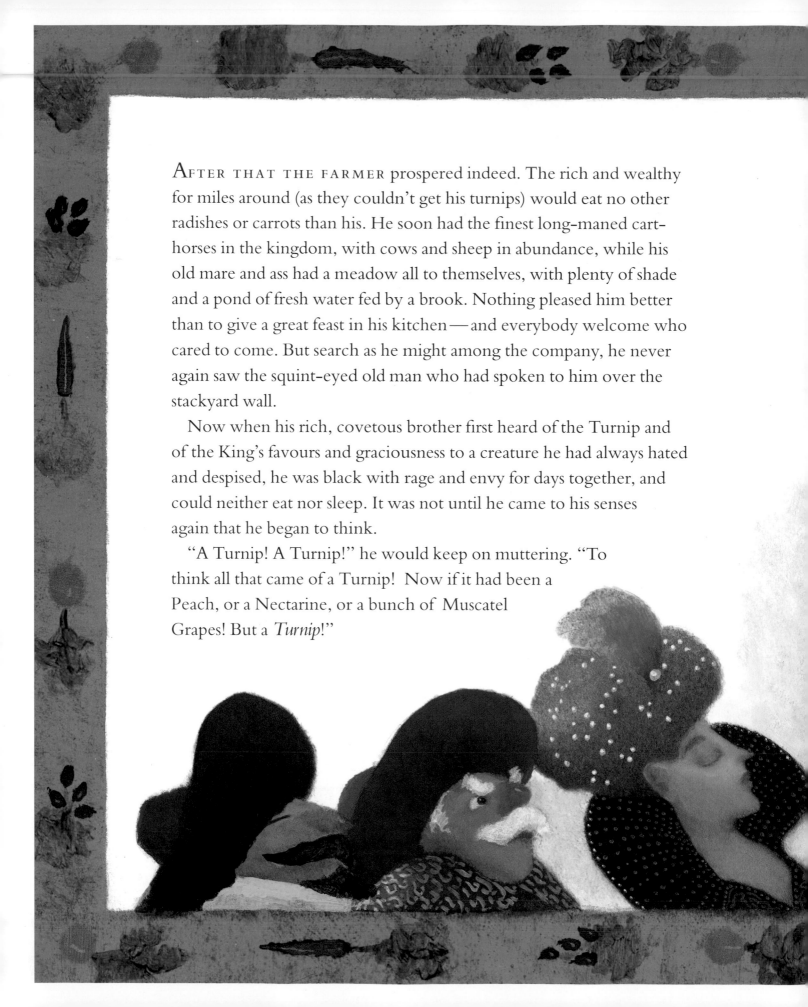

AFTER THAT THE FARMER prospered indeed. The rich and wealthy for miles around (as they couldn't get his turnips) would eat no other radishes or carrots than his. He soon had the finest long-maned carthorses in the kingdom, with cows and sheep in abundance, while his old mare and ass had a meadow all to themselves, with plenty of shade and a pond of fresh water fed by a brook. Nothing pleased him better than to give a great feast in his kitchen—and everybody welcome who cared to come. But search as he might among the company, he never again saw the squint-eyed old man who had spoken to him over the stackyard wall.

Now when his rich, covetous brother first heard of the Turnip and of the King's favours and graciousness to a creature he had always hated and despised, he was black with rage and envy for days together, and could neither eat nor sleep. It was not until he came to his senses again that he began to think.

"A Turnip! A Turnip!" he would keep on muttering. "To think all that came of a Turnip! Now if it had been a Peach, or a Nectarine, or a bunch of Muscatel Grapes! But a *Turnip*!"

THEN SUDDENLY A NOTION came into his head. He could scarcely breathe or see for a whole minute, it made him so giddy. Then he hastened out, got into his coach and went off to a certain rich city that was beyond the borders of his own country. There he sold nearly everything he possessed: his land, his jewels and gold plate, and most of his furniture. He even borrowed money on his fine house. Having by this means got all the cash he could, he went to the shop of a man who was a dealer in gems, and one celebrated in every country of the world.

There he bought the very largest ruby this man had to sell. It was clear and lustrous as crystal, red as pigeon's blood, and the size of an Evesham plum, but round as a marble. The man, poising it in a sunbeam between his finger and thumb, said there had never been a ruby to compare with it. This is a ruby, he said, fit only for a King.

Nothing could have pleased his customer better, though when the man went on to tell him the price of the gem his very heart seemed to turn inside out. Indeed, there was only just enough money in the three money-bags which the man's two shopmen had carried in for him to pay for it. But he thanked the man, put the little square box carefully into an inside pocket, stepped briskly into his coach and returned home.

NEXT DAY, IN HIS BEST CLOTHES, he went to the Palace and asked the Officer at the entry if the King would of his grace spare him but one, or, at most, two moments of his inestimable time. The Chamberlain returned and replied politely that his royal master desired to know who his visitor *was*. The rich man was made very hot and uncomfortable by this question. For the first time in his life he discovered that he didn't know. He knew what he *had* (most of it was now packed into the ruby in his pocket). He knew what he thought of himself; but he didn't know what he *was*. It was no use telling the King's Chamberlain his name, since he felt sure the King had never heard of it; he might just as well say "Uzzywuzzybub," or "Oogoowoogy."

The only thing he could think to say — and it tasted as horrid as a black draught when he said it — was that when he was a child he had been allowed by his father to play with the boy who was now the farmer who had brought the King the Turnip — which was just as much the whole truth as the rind of an orange is a whole orange.

When the King heard this he was so much amused that, sitting there in his Presence Chamber, he almost laughed aloud. He had guessed at once who his visitor was, for after enquiring about his beloved farmer (for beloved by everybody who knew him he truly was) he had heard much of this rich man — his half-brother. He knew what a mean skinflint he was, how he had robbed the poor and cheated the rich, and what kind of help he had given the farmer when he grievously needed it. And last, the King guessed well what he had now come for — to curry favour, and in hope of a reward. So he determined to teach this bad man a lesson.

WHEN WITH HIS RUBY HE APPEARED trembling, bowing, cringing and ducking before him, the King smiled on him saying, that if he had known his visitor was a friend of the farmer who grew the Turnip, he would have been at once admitted into his presence.

The rich man, having swallowed this bitter pill as best he could, bowed low once more, his fat cheeks like mulberries.

The King then asked him his business. So, without more ado, the rich man fetched out of a secret pocket of his gown the casket which contained the man's ruby, and with an obeisance to the very ground presented it to the King.

Now, though the farmer's Turnip, as turnips go, was such as no monarch in the world's history had ever seen before, this ruby, as Kings' rubies go, was not. But even if it had been, it would have made no difference to the King. To him it was not the gift that mattered, but the giver. Besides, he knew exactly why this rich man had come with his gem, and what he hoped to get out of it.

He smiled, he glanced graciously at the ruby, and said it was indeed a pretty thing. He then went on to tell his visitor that the prince, his small son, was not only fond of sitting on a farm wagon among the green tops of the biggest turnip there ever was, but also delighted in all kinds of col- oured beads, stones, glass, marbles, crystals, and quartz and that his young eyes in particular would be overjoyed at the sight of this new bauble. Then he raised his face, looked steadily at his visitor, and asked him what favour he could confer on him in return and as a mark of his bounty.

THE RICH MAN SHIVERED ALL OVER with joy; he didn't know where to look; he opened his mouth like a fish, then, like a fish, shut it again. At last he managed to blurt out that even the very smallest thing the King might be pleased to bestow on him would fill him with endless rapture. For so he hoped to get ten times more than he would have dared to ask.

The King smiled again, and said that, since the rich man could not choose for himself, the only thing possible would be to send him something which he himself greatly valued. "Ay," said he, "beyond words."

The rich man returned to his half-empty house overjoyed at the success of his plan. He was so proud of himself and so scornful of the mean people in the streets and the shopkeepers at their doors, that wherever he looked he squinted and saw double. For the next two days he could hardly eat or sleep. He had only one thought, "What will His Majesty send me?"

He fancied a hundred things and coveted all. Every hour of daylight he sat watching at his window, and the moment he drowsed off in his chair at night, he woke at what he thought was the sound of wheels. As for the only servant he now had left, the poor creature was worn to a skeleton, and hadn't an instant's peace.

On the third morning, as the rich man sat watching, his heart all but ceased to beat. A scarlet trumpeter on a milk-white charger came galloping down the street. The rich man hastened out to meet him, and was told that a gift from the King was even now on its way. Sure enough, a few minutes afterwards there turned the corner an immense dray drawn by six of the royal piebald horses, with an outrider in the royal livery to each pair, while a multitude of the townsfolk followed after it huzzaing it on. Yet it approached so slowly that the rich man thought he would die of suspense. But when at last it reached his gates he hadn't long to linger.

THE GREAT CANVAS COVERING of the wagon was drawn back, and there, on an enormous dish, lay the King's present, something, as he had said, that he valued beyond words. It was a large handsome slice of the farmer's Turnip.

At sight of it, at sight of the people, the rich man paused a moment — then ran. He simply took to his heels and ran, and if, poor soul, he had not been so much overfed and overfat . . .

. . . he might be running to this day.